Oy Vey!

The Hilarious Guide to Yiddish Culture and Slang

Matthew Katzman

Acknowledgements

Huge shoutout to my Zaidy & Bubbie for teaching me the Yiddish language.

Thank you to Omer & Tani for their Hebrew insights.

Big thanks to Jess & Joe for helping me put together some of the best bits.

And thank you to all other friends & family for supporting me along the way.

About the Author:

Matthew is a budding screenwriter with a psychology background from Queen's University. Inspired by the rich tales and experiences of his 92-year-old Zaidy, Matthew embarked on a mission to breathe new life into the vibrant yet undervalued Yiddish language that played a significant role in his upbringing.

"Yiddish Slang 101" weaves personal family stories with hilarious and whimsical Yiddish expressions. He creates a tapestry of humor and cultural reverence that will delight readers of all backgrounds. While cherishing the traditions of his Zaidy and Bubbie, Matthew invites you to discover the infectious joy of Yiddish through his book.

Design Coordinator – Scott Schwartz

Cartoon Illustrator - Alex Stiube

Praise for Oy Vey! Yiddish Slang 101:

"Oy Vey: Yiddish Slang 101 by Matthew Katzman is like a warm bowl of matzah ball soup. It reminds us of the rich, quirky language of our youth, whilst introducing a new generation to the geshmake expressions of mame-loshn. This book surely deserves a spot on the shelves of every Jewish home right next to The Joys of Yiddish"
 - *Reb Noyekh, yiddishwithnoyekh.com*

"It has been said that a good Yiddish joke can't be translated and land the same. Matthew Katzman understood the assignment. It's about the feeling and nuance and flavor... All of which Katzman brings to Yiddish Slang 101. This is a 'must get' to have in your home - and a geshmak Gift!" - *Suzie Pollak Becker, @schmoozewithsuze (IG)*

Unlock Your Yiddish Journey with Exclusive Bonuses!

We're excited to offer you some incredible bonuses to enhance your Yiddish learning experience.

Bonus 1: Bubbies Brain Teasers - The Ultimate Yiddish Puzzle Book

Are you ready to put your Yiddish skills to the test? Dive into our exclusive puzzle book featuring word searches, trivia questions, crosswords, and more. Challenge yourself and discover just how Yiddish you really are!

Bonus 2: Yiddish Audiobook Narration

Yiddish is a language that's as much about the spoken word as it is about the written one. That's why we've included an audiobook narration of this book. Listening to Yiddish pronunciation is essential to grasp the nuances and authenticity of the language. Our narrator, Louis, not only provides clear pronunciation but also brings the colorful Yiddish characters to life with his brilliant voices for the comics.

The best part? You can get both of these amazing bonuses absolutely FREE! Here's how:

Option 1: Type the link below into your internet browser to access your bonuses:
yiddishslang.com/bonus

Option 2: Scan the QR code below with your phone's camera to instantly access your bonuses:

Table of Contents

///////////////////////////////////

Chapter One Yiddish 101 7

Chapter Two The Kvetcher's Lexicon 8

Chapter Three Yiddish Insults to Throw at Your Friends 15

Chapter Four The Art of the Argument 25

Chapter Five Slangin' Praise 28

Chapter Six Mishpocha Matters 35

Chapter Seven They Tried to Kill Us, We Won, Let's Eat! 40

Chapter Eight The Gift of Gab 46

Chapter Nine Slang from the Israelis 51

Chapter Ten Happy Holidays! 55

Chapter Eleven The *Provocative* Chapter 60

Chapter Twelve Yiddish Proverbs 69

Chapter Thirteen Yiddish Aphorisms 72

Chapter Fourteen Placing a Curse on Your Worst Enemy 74

Chapter Fifteen Jewish Jokes 76

Chapter Sixteen Yiddish Culture from the Silver Screen 80

Chapter Seventeen Yiddish Expressions to Live By 84

Chapter Eighteen Bits That Didn't Seem to Fit Anywhere Else 87

Conclusion 95

A Big Ol' Yiddish Glossary 96

Chapter One

YIDDISH 101

Once the language spoken by Jewish people all across Europe, Yiddish has now been labelled as a dying language. **Feh!** While fewer people are speaking it these days, the Yiddish language is one that is vibrant, whimsical, and has some of the funniest sounding words out there.

If you didn't know, Yiddish was the traditional language of eastern European Jews. Today, it is still spoken by some in Israel, North America, and a handful of European countries. This wonderfully expressive language originates from a German dialect mixed with Hebrew words and other languages here and there. Let me take you on a journey to show you some of the very best in Yiddish sayings and expressions.

I've made it my mission to make sure you come away feeling excited about the Yiddish language! And even if you're not, I know that my Zaidy and Bubbie will enjoy this book. I <u>really</u> want them to be proud of me.

So if you don't leave with anything from reading this, that's fine. As long as I am praised by my friends, family, and community, it will all be worth it!

DISCLAIMER: This book features elements from the Yiddish AND Hebrew languages, with pieces of Jewish culture mixed in. Many of these elements blend together and we didn't want to leave anything important out!

Chapter Two

THE KVETCHER'S LEXICON

"Jews don't sing and pray. They complain and eat."

Christian Borle as Tom Levitt, **SMASH**

I hope you know how much Jews love to complain. For us, there's never a bad time to be complaining. Whether it was about the conditions of the **shtetl**, the small villages where my ancestors lived in Eastern Europe, or hanging out in a luxurious Upper East side living room. There are always things that are bothering us.

Bupkis (Bup-Kiss) n. - One of those beautiful words that just rolls off the tongue. It sounds like exactly what it means: a whole lot of nothing. It is interestingly the title of SNL star Pete Davidson's show about his life. Really makes you think if the title was ironic or not.

Eppes a nudnik (Ep-Pes-Ah-Nood-Nick) - Something of a pest or an absolute nuisance. Think of the younger sibling who is relentless about getting your parents' phone so they can play *Subway Surfers*... or whatever the kids are into these days. Think I might've lost touch.

Fakakta (Fah-Kuck-Tah) adj. - Meaning ridiculous, annoying, frustrating. Stick this word in a sentence to elevate how aggravated a situation is making you feel. "I went to the bakery to buy a **challah** and all they had was the **fakakta** multigrain one! No raisins or nothing!"

Farshlepteh krenk (Far-Shlep-Tah-Krenk) n. - This term refers to someone or something that is a constant pain in the you-know-what... neck. "I'm just ready for the US election to be over. It's been such a **farshlepteh krenk** and I know I'm voting for Kanye."

Feh! (Feh) excl. - A way for one to express their disgust or distaste in an unnecessarily over-dramatic way. What you say when you enter a New York City bodega bathroom.

Fershtickt (Fur-Shtikt) adj. - A feeling of disgust that suddenly hits you. Like finding out how babies are made. Spoiler alert: it is gross!

Fershnickered (Ferr-Shnik-Erd) adj. - When you become so drunk you can't even get yourself up. I'm not ashamed to admit I've had a few nights like this (I'm kind of a bad boy). One time I had a little too much at the New Years Eve party and when I woke up, it was 2023.

- **NOTE:** If you're a member of my family, a future partner, or someone considering employing me, please don't let this definition reflect my character. My **fershnickered** days are mostly behind me.

Furshlugginer (Fur-Shlugge-Ner) adj. - Meaning worn-down, beat-up, and a piece of junk. In the animated film *Hercules (1997)*, Danny Devito plays Phil and drops **Furshlugginer** in reference to Achilles' heel: "That **Furshlugginer** heel of his! Barely gets nicked there once and kaboom!...he's history."

Kvetch (Kuh-Vetch) v. - This one is an absolute classic and the epitome of Yiddish slang. A person can be a **kvetcher** when they whine about how slow the traffic is moving, the weather, the rising cost of living, inefficient bureaucracy, etc.

Meshugganeh (Meh-Shoog-Ah-Neh) adj. - Someone who is crazy or insane. Can be used in a loving way in the right context but use it as an insult until further notice.

Mishegoss (Mish-Ooh-Guss) n. - Insanity, craziness, or all out madness.

Ongepotchket (Ohn-Geh-Poch-Ket) adj. - When something is tacky or overdone. Some Jewish people might think Rabbi jokes are **ongepotchket** but that's probably because they just haven't heard the right one.

Oy vey! (Oy-Vey) excl. - A vibrant response to when you hear something bad happening. "**Oy Vey!** She lost her place while reading her Bat Mitzvah portion!" or "**Oy Vey!** I just tried a new recipe for my kugel and let's just say it's a good thing takeout exists!"

Oy-yoy-yoy! (Oy-Yoy-Yoy) excl. - A step up from **Oy Vey!** When you hear of something REALLY bad.

My **dummkopf** friend: "I thought it was a legitimate clothing site and now I've been charged $300 for a pair of corduroys!"
Me: **Oy-yoy-yoy!**

Tzuris (Tsoo-Riss) n. - Meaning trouble. Imagine how much cooler that *Elvis* song would've been if he wrote it in Yiddish: "If you're looking for **tzuris**, you came to the right place. If you're looking for **tzuris**, take a look at my **punim** (face)."

Umbashrien (Oom-Bah-Shrine) excl. - An exclamation of "God forbid!". Us Jewish people have a lot of ways to **kvetch**.

Chapter Three

YIDDISH INSULTS TO THROW AT YOUR FRIENDS

"He may look like an idiot and talk like an idiot but don't let that fool you. He really is an idiot."

Groucho Marx

Have you ever met a person and thought, "If I looked up the word **schmuck** in the dictionary, I'd see your face"? Jewish people have some great words for insulting all kinds of people. Maybe it's because we're easily frustrated. Or maybe it's because we're surrounded by **nudniks.**

Alter kocher (Alter-Kawk-Err) n. - Literally translates to "old crapper". An old, miserable, poorly-mannered Jewish man. Usually has a thick yiddish accent. If you want to see what pure wrath and fury look like, say this to your dad at **Shabbat** dinner.

Farbisseneh punim (Far-Bissi-Neh-Poo-Nim) n. - An ugly, bitter, grouchy, and sour looking face.

Farshtinkener (Far-Shtin-Keh-Ner) n. - A person who smells bad. I once heard *Larry King* described as a **farshtinkener** and that feels like the perfect description.

Farchtunken (Farch-Toon-Ken) adj. - Something or someone that is nasty. This can pertain to their appearance, their personality, or their overall vibe. For example, everyone used to think Ellen Degeneres was a **mensch** (a good person) but it turned out she was yet another **farshtinkener,** described as "One of the meanest people alive" by a former writer.

Chazzer (Chah-Zerr) adj. - A piggish person. An absolute **zhlub**.

Klutz (Klutz) n. - A dope or a clumsy person. Maybe in your life it's the guy who spilled the freshly brewed pot of coffee all over his white shirt. Maybe it's your friend who always manages to trip over his feet at the worst times. Or maybe it's...you?

Mamzer (Mum-Zehr) n. - A dubious, bastardous kind of person. The term comes from the **Torah,** the Jewish Bible, and refers to a person who is literally born out of a forbidden relationship.

Fershimmeled (Fur-Shimm-Uld) adj. - To be confused, in a tizzy, or all out discombobulated. Like when you walk into a room and immediately forget why you entered the room. This happens to me all the time. Sometimes I remember that I was looking for my keys. Other times, I remember that I was supposed to turn off the stove. Sorry Bubbie, but your barbecue brisket is gonna come out a little <u>too</u> well done.

Makhasheyfe (Mach-Hah-Shay-Feh) n. - A witch of a woman. Sometimes it is used to refer to one's mother-in-law, but I would never do such a thing.

Nochshlepper (Noch-Shlep-Per) n. - That unwanted person who tags along in your friend group, laughs at jokes they don't understand, and brings a very weird vibe. I tend to feel bad for the **nocheshelpper** but I also don't want them around. It's a delicate dichotomy.

Nogoodnik (No-Good-Nick) n. - A person who is good for absolutely nothing. Not my words but I've heard my **Bubbie** refer to the Kardashians as **Nogoodniks** since no one really understands why they're famous or what their point is.

Nudnik (Nood-Nick) n. - An annoying pest of a person, who doesn't really think before they act. It can be fun to be a **nudnik** in some situations but never at jury duty.

Paskudnyak (Pas-Kood-Nick) n. - A nasty, revolting, and disgusting individual. Someone you absolutely cannot stand. For me, it's this kid named Shlomi who I used to go to high school with. He is pretty much every word in this chapter rolled up into one. I hope you never have to meet him. But if you do, you'll know.

Putz (Putz) n. - An easily manipulated and gullible person. The kind of person who falls for just about every trick in the book. My friend Rafi can be quite the **putz** and some of his friends like to play little pranks on him. One time he was tricked into believing that our friends crossed the border, bought a dog, and were forced to give it up when they crossed back. He was devastated that he never got to meet Spot.

Schmuck (Shmuck) n. - A perfect word to describe an all-out fool. This term has firmly entered into mainstream English to encapsulate the biggest dummies out there. For example, Steve Carell and Zach Galifinakis play absolute **schmucks** in the aptly titled film, *Dinner for Schmucks (2010).* It's a great movie about the power of friendship, not judging a book by its cover, and learning to accept yourself. Highly recommend checking it out after you finish this chapter.

Shande (Shon-Deh) n. - An absolute disgrace. Your Jewish parents may call you this when you decide to pursue writing instead of medicine or law. Oops!

Schmendrik (Shmen-Drick) n. - A weak, foolish, nincompoop. When I think of true **schmendricks**, I like to think of Derek Zoolander from *Zoolander (2001)*. While he is especially stupid, like a true **shmendrik**, he is still incredibly endearing.

Shmoe (Shmoe) n. - Someone who is a mark for telemarketers. An absolute dummo. But not quite as gullible as a **putz**.

Tuchas leker (Too-Chas-Leh-Ker) n. - A kiss-ass. That annoying co-worker who loves going to work everyday and praises your **chazzerish** boss.

Zhlub (Zhlub) n. - Someone with poor manners. One could call them a slob. I'd just call them my brother! Just kidding Benny we all love you but would it kill you to take a shower every now and then?!

Shlumperdik (Shlum-Per-Dick) adj. - One who is messy, sloppy, and unclean. This is a good word to describe your college roommate. The kinda guy who leaves apples in mysterious locations around your dorm room or sleeps on a pile of unwashed clothes.

The Difference Between a Schlemiel and Schlimazel

Schlemiel and Schlimazel are famous comedic Yiddish archetypes that appear frequently in many of their stories. They almost always interact, facing unfortunate, yet differing circumstances.

Schlemiel (Schleh-Meal) n. - This is the type of character who is prone to accidents. You may read about them tripping over their feet, falling on their face, or dropping a hot bowl of soup.

Schlimazel (Schleh-Mah-Zul) n. - The schlimazel is the unfortunate recipient of the schlemiel's clumsiness. You may read about them getting a hot bowl of soup poured in their lap from a falling Schlemiel.

For example, in *Seinfeld*, George Constanza often plays the **schlemiel**, while Jerry acts as the **schlimazel**. In one episode, George loses his glasses, believing to then see Jerry's new girlfriend kissing Jerry's cousin, Jeffery. Jerry eventually confronts her, resulting in them breaking up. In the end, it turned out that what George was really seeing was a police officer kissing its horse.

Chapter Four

THE ART OF THE ARGUMENT

"Two Jews, three opinions."

Sandee Brawarsky & Deborah Mark

Arguing is a Jewish birthright and here are some words to help you win one. We love to argue and we might even argue about how we don't like to argue. Many of these arguments begin with harmless discussions that evolve into fun debates and eventually vigorous disputes. Which is fine, as long as you don't suggest that someone's wife is a **makhasheyfe.** In that case, you'd be venturing into Chapter three territory.

Dummkopf (Doom-Koff) n. - A stupid, blockhead, dingus, lunk, moron, lunatic, imbecile, halfwit, nincompoop, numbskull, fool, dimwit, **putz**, dummy. A perfect way to tie these terms together.

Fonferer (Fawn-Fur-Err) n. - The kind of person who talks through their nose and out their ass, as my dad would say. They act like they know so much more than you. In reality, they probably read a few tweets or did a quick read-up on Wikipedia. Look out for **fonferers** on such topics as: war, AI, cryptocurrency, anything politics, daylight savings, gun control, homework, immigration, milk consumption,

GMOs, student loan, and fruit rankings.

Hitsiger (Hit-Sig-Err) n. - One who is a hothead. These individuals are a cork waiting to burst or an ax-head ready to fly off the handle. In Jewish culture, these tend to be old, grumpy men. Many of them you'll find at synagogue, sitting in the corner, and pouting. It's hard to know what their next move is so it's best to just avoid them.

Karger (Karr-Gerr) n. - One who is a penny pincher. Someone who refuses to spend a single dollar if they're able to. This is unfortunately one of the most persistent and prominent Jewish stereotypes. Therefore, I must do everything in my power to disprove this, even if that means spending $9 for a hot dog at Dodger Stadium instead of bringing food from home.

Pisher (Pish-Err) - To call someone a child in the sense that they are very inexperienced. Literally translates to "bed wetter". Add the word *little* in front to really lay it on thick. "Wow! You think you're such a **big macher** but in reality you're just a **little pisher**."

Pisk (Pisk) n. - The kind of person who just won't shut up. You'll see this is a common theme in Jewish culture and Yiddish slang. Jewish people just loveeee to talk about anything and everything. Maybe it's something deeply personal that you did not originally intend to share. Maybe it's something profoundly uninteresting that no one cares to hear. In any case, the **pisk** is relentless.

Schnorrer (Shnor-Err) n. - One who is a big moocher, beggar, or freeloader. The kind of person who takes without directly stealing. Your girlfriend can be a bit of a **schnorrer** when you go out for dinner and she asks for just one bite of your burger. She ordered the salad and you can tell she deeply regrets her decision. One bite then turns into two and before you know it, she's housed half the thing! If she wanted a burger, she could've just ordered one. I'm sorry to call you out like this, Emily, but it's ridiculous.

THE ART OF THE ARGUMENT

Chapter Five

SLANGIN' PRAISE

*"I **love** everyone! I **love** to be around some people, I **love** to stay away from others, and some I'd **love** to punch in the face."*

*Unknown (probably some **yenta**)*

Despite all the nasty insults you can throw at someone, there's also gotta be a way to tell someone they're doing a good job. After all, everyone knows at least a **mensch** or two.

Chevrusa (Chev-Roo-Sah) n. - A friendship or a companion. It can also refer to the pairings that Jewish students and scholars may study in.

Chutzpah (Chuts-Pah) n. - A frequently used word that has really entered the mainstream, meaning a high level of boldness or confidence. Make sure to <u>really</u> pronounce that "ch" sound. Might require an adequate amount of phlegm in the back of your throat.

Kvell (Kvell) v. - To absolutely burst with pride for something. Your **Bubbie** might say she was absolutely **kvelling** watching you deliver your Torah portion.

L'Chaim! (Luh-Chai-Im) excl. - Meaning, "To life!". Used when one is giving a toast to one's health, success, or well-being. Famously sung about in the 1971 musical drama, *Fiddler on the Roof*, after the main character's daughter is engaged to be married. Also famously sung by the Black Eyed Peas on *I Gotta Feeling (2009)*, making it a Bar and Bat Mitzvah party classic for decades to come.

Farputst (Far-Putst) adj. - Someone who is a very nice dresser or who's got crazy style. If you want to see someone with great Jewish style, look up Yosel Tiefenbrun, a **rebbe** who was written about in *GQ* for his "insane drip".

Geshmak (Geh-Shmack) adj. - Said about something that is delicious, fun, or pleasurable. Often used to describe a meal. My Bubbie's specialty is a dish called *Nalysnyky*, a thin crepe that is a common Russian dish. They are indeed **geshmak.**

Mensch (Mensh) n. - Literally translates to "a person". Has come to mean a <u>good</u> person. Someone who operates with honor and integrity, or does good deeds for others (these deeds are also known as *mitzvahs*).

In middle school, they used to hand out something called "The **Mensch** Award", given to the person who is the kindest throughout the entire year. Unfortunately, I put off being a nice person until the end of the year. By then it was too late and it went to some guy named Justin. Lesson learned: you can't cram good deeds.

Naches (Na-Chess) n. - The pride you feel for someone but in a lesser manner than a kvell. Not to be confused with *nachos*, a traditional Mexican dish that consists of fried corn tortilla chips usually topped with cheese, meat, and sour cream. This is a Yiddish book after all.

Pishkeh (Pish-Keh) n. - An underdog or undersized champ. David was the original **pishkeh** in the fight against Goliath. But the modern-day **pishkeh** has to be 5"9 NBA player Nate Robinson, who somehow blocked the shot of 7"6 Yao Ming back in 2006. Height doesn't measure heart!

Yiddishe kop (Yid-Dish-Eh-Kop) n. - Someone who has a scholarly brain. Would make a great **chevrusa** partner.

Zeyer sheyn gezogt (Zair-Shayn-Ge-Zuh-Gt) excl. - When someone says something you agree with, you reply with this phrase, meaning "well put!"

Chapter Six

MISHPOCHA MATTERS

"I'm very loyal in a relationship. Any relationship. When I go out with my mom, I don't look at other moms and go, "I wonder what her macaroni and cheese tastes like."

Garry Shandling

Family is important to everyone. But for the Jewish people, it's ingrained into culture, tradition, and religion. Family is always there for you and we have plenty of names to refer to these...honestly, annoying people. As much as I love my Bubbie and Zaidy, I don't love being asked about relationship status, career goals, or whatever else is going wrong in my life.

Baleboste (Bah-Leh-Boos-Teh) n. - A first-rate homemaker. Someone who cooks, cleans, and looks after the family.

Bashert (Bah-Shert) n. - Meaning "what's meant to be", often used to describe one's true love. The person you were destined to be with. For some, it might be their high school sweetheart. For others, someone they met later in life. It could even be a cat, dog, mouse, bird, fish, or snake.

Bubbie (Buh-Bee) n. - This is the grandmother of a family. The **Bubbie** keeps **Zaidy,** the grandfather, in check at all times. For example, when **Zaidy** says something insulting to his grandson, the **Bubbie** gives him an elbow to the ribs and he immediately understands that it's time to apologize.

Chuch/Chuchie (Chuch/Chuh-Chee) n. - This is a term of endearment and nickname usually for one's grandchild. It can also be used to represent anyone who feels like a family member.

Gantzeh mispocha (Gant-Seh-Mish-Poh-Chah) n. - Literally meaning the whole family. Can also be used to mean a friend group, aka your figurative family.

Tatelah (Tah-Te-Leh) n. - Literally meaning "little papa" but used to describe a well behaved child.

Mamaloshen (Mama-Loh-Shen) n. - The mother tongue. This can refer to someone who speaks Yiddish in a cool and fun way, expertly incorporating slang they may have learned from this lil' book.

Shayna punim (Shay-Nah-Puh-Num) n. - Meaning pretty face. From my experience at least, this has been used to describe a cute child by an annoying Jewish relative at a family function. It is always followed by a non-consensual pinch of your cheeks.

Zaidy (Zay-Dee) n. - The grandfather. The Zaidy is almost always a **nudnik** who tries all sorts of **meshugas**. The **Zaidy** tends to be impulsive too. He may say he's in good enough shape to play football with the extended family, only to break his hip trying the slickest spin move since Uncle Mordecai back in 2015.

Based on a true story.

Chapter Seven

THEY TRIED TO KILL US, WE WON, LET'S EAT!

"Ask not what you can do for your country. Ask what's for lunch."

Orson Welles

Food is a major component of any Jewish holiday, family gathering, or event in general. Have you ever been to one of these functions? Jewish people will fill you to the brim with the most outrageous **nosh** you have ever had. I'm talking about **kugel**. I'm talking about **matzo ball soup**. Maybe a few **sufganiyot** on *Hanukkah* or a hearty **cholent** at your **Shabbos** meal.

Curious about the title of this chapter? The history behind most Jewish holidays follow this chronology: a powerful leader tried to eliminate the Jewish people, they failed, and in commemoration, we eat delicious food!

Bissel (Biss-Uhl) n. - This refers to a small piece, a bit, or a little. Traditionally refers to a small quantity of food. You may say to your **Bubbie**, "I only want a **bissel** of your barbecue brisket", but she will most certainly give you the largest portion your eyes have ever seen... and then guilt you if you can't finish it.

Bubaleh (Bub-Ah-Leh) n. - This is a big, matzah pancake made during the holiday of *Passover*. Served with maple syrup, jam, chocolate spread, or whatever other sweet toppings you can get your hands on. The phrase has been co-opted as a term of endearment for someone you love. Traditionally used to describe a cute child or grandchild.

Cholent (Choh-Lent) n. - A traditional stew that is often served on **Shabbos**, the Jewish day of rest. This stew is made the night before and left to simmer for 10-12 hours. This is because the rules of **Shabbos** forbid any type of work to be done. This term can also be used to describe an attractive, older person because, like a traditional cholent, it has been cooking for a long time but still keeps all the flavor.

THEY TRIED TO KILL US, WE WON, LET'S EAT!

Hamantaschen (Hah-Men-Taw-Shen) n. - A delicious triangle pastry that is made and eaten during the Jewish holiday of *Purim*. These special treats are filled with a variety of jams, poppy seeds, or chocolate. The desert is created to symbolize the hat of the villain of the story, *Haman*, who tried and failed to kill the Jewish people in Persia. Therefore, we eat and destroy his ugly, symbolic hat.

Ibbegeblibenis (Ib-Beh-Ge-Blib-Eh-Ness) n. - Meaning leftovers. I recently learned this word and I have to say, it is probably the toughest one to sound out. Try saying it ten times fast.

Kashe-bulbe (Kah-Sheh-Bull-Beh) n. - This one refers to mashed potatoes. You can't write a full chapter on Jewish food without mentioning some form of potatoes. They are an essential ingredient for so many Jewish dishes like latkes, **kugel**, bourekas, **cholent**, etc. It is more importantly an incredibly fun word to say. Want to test the sanity of your family members? Repeat it over and over during your West Coast road trip and watch as their mental health quickly unravels.

Kishkas (Kish-Kahs) n. - This dish is beef intestines stuffed with a variety of meats, potatoes, grains, and vegetables. Because of its *unique* casing, it can be used to refer to a courageous, gutsy individual. My friend Adam decided to move to Israel all by himself. The guy has **kishkas**.

Kugel (Kuh-Gul) n. - A baked casseroles that comes in many styles and cooked for various holidays. Most famous being potato **kugel**.

Matzo Ball Soup (Matzah-Ball-Soop) n. - This is one of the greatest creations known to man. A dish that has been shown to heal all mental and physical wounds. It is like a warm hug inside your stomach.

Nosh (Naw-Sh) v. or n. - Refers to when you just want a snack or a little nibble of something. To your mother, a **nosh** might be the kind of thing to spoil your dinner. To your father, a **nosh** is his stash of candy that he hides from everyone else and eats periodically. To you, it is whatever you can get your hands on from dad's stash before he catches you.

Sufganiyot (Soof-Gah-Nee-Yot) n. - A jelly donut that is eaten during the Jewish holiday of *Hanukkah*. During this holiday, we eat oily foods to symbolise the scarce amount of oil in the Temple miraculously lasting eight days.

Rugelach (Roo-Gah-Lach) n. - This is another heavenly baked good. It is not associated with a Jewish holiday and can luckily be eaten at any time. It is similar in shape and style to a croissant but better in my honest opinion.

Schmaltz (Shmaltz) n. - Refers to rendered goose or chicken fat. Slang for when something is performative, sappy, and over-the-top. A few weeks ago I saw my cousin's middle-school performance of *Romeo and Juliet*. The **schmaltz** was thick to say the least. A lot of his peers were real amateurs but at least he played a great *Mercutio*.

Appropriate Topics at Shabbos Dinner

Every Friday night, we gather with family and friends for a festive meal, known as **Shabbos** (or Shabbat). While this dinner is supposed to be pleasant and relaxing, the wrong topic can turn things sour. Especially if you have cousins with some controversial opinions (looking at you, Nathan). To help you out, I've prepared some discussion topics that will help you avoid controversy, ensuring an enjoyable evening:

- Favorite character from *The Wire (2002)*
- Best speed to walk at (i.e., slow, medium, medium-fast, fast, super-fast)
- The Louisiana Purchase
- Ranking of the *Stranger Things* kids
- Worst things to smell (e.g., sewers, rotten food)
- Best Jeopardy host after Trebek
- The 2003 invasion of Iraq
- Where do you buy your pants from?
- Should they reboot *Jon & Kate Plus 8*?
- Pluto: planet or not?
- The Tonya Harding incident
- Best pet
- Climate change: good or bad?

Chapter Eight

THE GIFT OF GAB

"Do I have to say hello AND goodbye? Why do I have to say both?!"

Larry David

Have you ever caught two Jews who haven't seen each other in a while reuniting? It is a sight to see. The degree of **schmoozing** that goes on is outrageous. Two **yentas** yapping at one another in the deli aisle of your local grocery store is the best place to find it.

Ferklempt (Fur-Klempt) adj. - When one feels too overwhelmed to even talk. But not too overwhelmed to say the word **ferklempt**. It seems a bit contradictory but don't think about it too much.

Kibbitz (Kib-Itz) v. - To mindlessly gab and chat away, sometimes in pursuit of juicy gossip. My Aunt Maude always comes to family functions with that same look in her eye, ready to corner someone and **kibbitz** them for hours. That's how she gets all her insider information.

Schmooze (Shuh-Mooze) v. - To talk to someone in a friendly or vibrant way; to be a social butterfly. One is a **schmoozer** when they go to a party and try to talk to every person there. **Schmoozers** don't tend to care if they make a fool of themselves, they just want to make some new friends.

Mazel tov! (Mah-Zul-Tohv) excl. - A way of expressing congratulations to someone. May be used at weddings, bar/bat mitzvahs, holidays, or maybe even the funeral of your mortal enemy. Actually scratch that last one, I don't want to give Shlomi the satisfaction.

Nu? (Noo). excl. - In general, meaning "so what?", in slang to say "Out with it already!".

Tachlis (Tach-Liss) n. - To speak openly and bluntly. You could say, "Let's talk tachlis" meaning let's get down to business.

Yenta (Yen-Tah) n. - A gossiper. So much worse than a **kibbitzer**. The **yenta** cannot keep their mouth shut to save their life. I've known so many **yentas** in my time. For example, your friend when they spoil the ending of *The Sixth Sense* for you. Or your mom when she tells her friends that even at age 12, you still wet the bed, because you had an immature bladder.

Yutz/Yutzi (Yutz/Yutz-Ee) n. - A social outcast. Someone who is awkward in almost every single social situation they're in. I have a surprising amount of friends who I'd call **Yutzi**. When it's just you two hanging out, they're the coolest dudes. But when you take them to a party, they stand in the corner like a mime at a rock concert.

Chapter Nine

SLANG FROM THE ISRAELIS

"There is a difference between Israelis and Jews. Israelis, each and every one of them, gets drafted into the service. Jews, we complain about a draft to the service: 'Waiter, is there a vent open? I feel something blowing on my shoulder.'"

Elon Gold

While many of our people fled Europe for the great American dream, some of them went on to Israel, *the Holy Land*. Here, they spent decades crafting a unique Jewish culture, with their own language and slang.

Achalti otah (Ah-Chall-Tee-Oh-Tah) expr. - Literally meaning "I ate it". Used for when you miss out on something or someone screwed you over.

Achi (Ah-Chee) n. - Brother or bro, but in a deep sense. The passionate connection two men share in a *totally* heterosexual way.

Arss (Arr-Ss) n. - This is what you'd call a frat boy, asshole, or douchebag. In Israel, you'll see these dudes walking around blasting music on a speaker, wearing tank tops and chains, and being rambunctious.

Balagan (Bah-La-Gan) n. - A term that is used when things go all to hell. An absolute mess of sorts. A wreck of sheer chaos!

Benzonah (Ben-Zoh-Nah) adj. - A serious curse word, referring to someone or something as a son-of-a-b*tch. But it can also be used in a positive sense. "Damn, this shawarma is **benzonah!**"

Beimaschah (Beh-Ee-Mash-Chah) expr. - Translates to "on your mother". Used when someone says something unbelievable, that they have to swear on their mother's name that it is real. Like when you're at the club and the most beautiful girl you ever laid your eyes on asks if you can set her up with your dinky friend.

Chachlah (Chach-Lah) n. - A selfish, bratty, and dim-witted girl. This is the female equivalent of an **arss**. In Israel, you'll see these gals really going for it with their makeup and big hair, strutting around.

Doogri (Doo-Gree) expr. - Meaning "to be completely honest...", followed by a true statement. The Israeli equivalent of "tbh".

Kaliber (Kah-Lee-Berr) adj. - When someone is really good or spot on with something.

Leetafetz (Lee-Tah-Fetz) adj. - To feel so tired that your eyes keep shutting. Have you ever been to a party with a bunch of business majors and end up talking about the latest blockchain technology? Exactly like that.

Mah ani ez?! (Mah-Ah-Nee-Yez) excl. - Literally translating to, "What am I, a goat?". It is when someone overlooks or passes you over something you felt entitled to. My **Zaidy's** equivalent would be, "What am I, chopped liver?". He also really enjoys eating chopped liver so it's a bit of a head scratcher.

Noder (Noh-Derr) n. or v. - In Judaism, there are different levels of vows in the **Torah**, ranking from the most basic to most important. This is the highest level that one can vow or swear. With that being said, this can be used in any kind of context. You can **noder** to your sister that you didn't eat the last cookie. You can **noder** to your mom that you completed your homework. You can **noder** to yourself that, despite the controversial past of your favorite musician, you can separate the art from the artist.

Sababa (Sah-Buh-Buh) adj. - Meaning it's all good in the hood. Israelis use this term for almost anything. Despite missiles flying in and out every so often, things are almost always **sababa.**

Sachi (Sah-Chee) n. - Someone who is outrageously uninteresting and a prude. The type of person who watches *Friends* reruns over and over, making it a part of their personality.

Ya wah adi (Yah-Woo-Ah-Dee) excl. - Oh wow! Oh my god!

Yalla! (Yah-La) excl. - An Arabic word that has firmly entered the Israeli language, meaning "Let's go!". One of the most common terms that you will hear if you're there. It appears in every other sentence for native Israelis. That's because it is incredibly versatile. For example, it can be used when someone is:

- Angry: "Let's get a move on!"
- Excited: "Let's gooooo [team]!"
- To start something: "Let's get going!"
- In terrible Tel Aviv traffic: "Cmon, let's go!"
- ...and many more.

Some Israelis like to end conversations with "**Yalla,** bye". They can be a very blunt people.

Chapter Ten

HAPPY HOLIDAYS!

"Shabbat shalom, motherf***ers."

Adam Goldberg as Mordechai Jefferson Carver, **The Hebrew Hammer**

In Judaism, holidays are of tremendous significance. We use these times to get together with our community to celebrate, commemorate, or reflect. Prayers are often followed by a gargantuan meal, where you'll get to hear about your relatives' crazy politics. Pro tip: don't bring up the upcoming election unless you want to see Aunt Sophie fling her Matzo Ball at Uncle Everett.

Chag sameach (Chag-Suh-May-Ach) excl. - Meaning happy holidays! The greeting to give your friends, family, and community at the festive meal.

Gut yontif (Goot-Yon-Teef) excl. - Used as a greeting to welcome in the holidays.

Gmar chatima toyva (Gamar-Cha-Tee-Mah-Toy-Va) excl. - A phrase said to someone on the holiday of Yom Kippur, meaning may you be sealed in the book of life. On Yom Kippur, Jewish people fast to reflect and repent of their sins and ask for forgiveness. The expression is ultimately a way of saying "Good luck starving for the next 25 hours."

Mohel (Moy-Ell) n. - This is the title of the person who does the *snip snip* at a **bris**, also known as a circumcision. Apparently at my **bris**, my dad's best friend passed out after seeing *the snipping*. Didn't have the **kishkas** I guess.

Rebbe (Reh-Bee) n. - This is the yiddish way of saying the Rabbi. A **rebbe's** job is to lead the congregation at a synagogue through prayer services and religious teachings. **Rebbes** are like rock stars in a lot of ways: they play to huge crowds, are adored by their fans, their performances are constantly scrutinized, and they make a lot more money than you'd think.

Shana tova (Shah-Nah-Toy-Vah) excl. - Meaning, "Happy New Year!". Because the Hebrew calendar is based on the moon, our new year, known as *Rosh Hashanah*, comes in September. Instead of popping champagne and counting down to midnight, we get together with our family to eat apples with honey.

Shofar (Shoh-Far) n. - This is a musical horn that is blown in Synagogue on such holidays as *Rosh Hashanah* and *Yom Kippur* at the end of the service. There are many biblical reasons as to why we blow the **shofar** in synagogue but I like to think it's to wake up the people who fell asleep.

Simchah (Seem-Chah) n. - Any joyous celebration of a festive occasion. This could refer to a wedding, bar mitzvah, **bris**, etc.

Tizku leshanim rabot (Teez-Ku-Leh-Shah-Neem-Rah-Bot) excl. - Wishing someone many good years to come!

Sh'koyech (Sheh-Koy-Ach) excl. - To say "More power to you!" or "Good job!". Often said after someone reads the Torah.

Surviving Your Yom Kippur Fast

Every year in September, *Rosh Hashanah*, the Jewish new year, rolls around. This is a fun time to be a Jewish person. We get to eat an assortment of fun foods like: apples with honey, challah, pomegranates, cakes, and an assortment of desserts.

Ten days after the New Year comes *Yom Kippur*, the day of atonement. *Yom Kippur* could not be more opposite to *Rosh Hashanah*. During this "holiday", you are not supposed to bathe, brush your teeth, wear perfumes, wear leather, or eat for 25 hours. This is to repent and ask for forgiveness from those we have wronged.

This day of fasting can be quite difficult, leaving many Jews wondering how to make it through. Having successfully completed this fast every year since my bar mitzvah in 2013, I will give you some of the tips that have helped me through.

1) *Sleep as much as you can* - If you're not conscious, you can't feel hungry.

2) *Think about the least appetising thing you can* - For me, it's the sheets on the grandparents' shared bed in *Willy Wonka and the Chocolate Factory*.

3) *Watch a good movie* - Last year, I watched *Shutter Island* and the year before that I watched *Avatar*. Intense stories with three hour run times are your best friend.

4) *Stay away from hangry people* - Hangry = hungry + angry. People who get hangry will usually unleash hell upon you if you breathe in the wrong way.

5) *Avoid locations where people aren't fasting* - There are many reasons people may not fast, like for health, medication-related, different religious values, etc. All totally valid. But if you smell a grilled cheese sizzling in the pan when you've been fasting, it's gonna make things <u>much</u> tougher.

And with that, good luck! Just try to use your time fasting to reflect on how you can be better in the next year and not on how f**king hungry you are.

Chapter Eleven

THE *PROVOCATIVE* CHAPTER

"My sister was with two men in one night...She could hardly walk after that. Can you imagine? Two dinners? That's a lot of food."

Sarah Silverman

This chapter is NOT for the faint of heart. Prepare to hear some of the most foul, noxious, repugnant terms you've ever heard. Just kidding, it's mostly about mild sex stuff.

Erotoman (Erah-Tow-Munn) adj. - This is what we'd call someone who has a sex addiction. Considered by some to be the coolest kind of addiction. But I don't think any addictions are cool. I'm a really good person.

Eynnakhtl (Ayn-Nacht-Tull) n. - Nothing wrong with a little one-night stand. Or as I like to call it, "A **shtup** and skedaddle".

Gikhele (Gich-Eh-Leh) n. or v. - This is to have a quickie. You know, when you're rushing to get to family dinner but you wanna get all those hormones out. Hop in a bathroom stall, get in the backseat of your car, or find a vacant mausoleum. All equally great options.

Kish mir in tuchas (Kish-Meer-In-Too-Chas) excl. - This expression translates to telling someone to kiss your ass. An exquisite phrase for those looking to add a touch of whimsy to their verbal repertoire.

Libe-feter (Leeb-Eh-Feh-Ter) n. - A sugar daddy. If you're not familiar, this is the kind of older man who buys expensive gifts for younger women in exchange for her company or for sexual favors. I'd personally prefer to use this term to refer to *Willy Wonka*. In many ways, he's a kind of candy father to all those who enter his chocolate factory.

BONUS CHAPTER

Jewish Pick-Up Lines

Onknipverter (Ohn-Kneep-Ver-Ter) n. - What is known as a pickup line, those little phrases used to hit on someone.

Here are some good examples you can use to hopefully find your **bashert**:

1) Is your father *HaShem*? Because you're the answer to all my prayers.
2) Are you the oil from the *Hanukkah* story? Because you'd make me last eight days.
3) Are you a *yarmulke* (religious cap)? Because you're making me feel blessed and protected in your presence.
4) If you were a *mitzvah*, you'd be the most fulfilling one I've ever done.
5) Are you a *Torah*? Because I want to explore your depths and find meaning in your words.
6) (And finally) Do you believe in love at first **shofar**? Or should I blow it again?

Please try these and let me know how they go. So far I'm 0 for 8 but I think that says less about the quality of the lines and more about the character of the ladies hearing them.

Potch in tuchas (Poch-Een-Too-Chas) excl. - A slap on the behind. Interestingly, it has a very different meaning from a kiss on the ass. This is the kind of thing athletes do to tell each other they did a good job. I think it's just an excuse for two men to touch each other's butts.

Polutsye (Poh-Loot-Syeh) n. - What is known as a wet dream. I hope I don't have to give you another anatomy lesson here. If you're so curious, you can look it up after finishing this chapter.

Shtup (Shtup) n. or v. - Sexual intercourse! This term is generally used in a very casual way: "Did you hear Jeremy **shtupped** that girl from the bar last night? Apparently used a Jewish pickup line he learned from some cool, new book."

Tsutsiik (Tsoo-Tseek) n. - An attractive, hot, and sexy individual. "Wow, that Ella girl from my Philosophy class is **Tsutsiik**. I should try one of the pickup lines I learned from this scintillating Yiddish book I've been reading."

Tuchas (Too-Chas) - Ass, butt, anus...you get the picture.

Words for 'penis' - There's something about the male genitals that resonate with the Jewish people. Maybe it's the funky shape. Maybe it's something Freudian. Regardless of the reason, here are some of my favorites: **pecker, petseleh, petzl, schlong, schmekel, schmok, shtupper, shvantz.**

Zi hot farflokhtn a koyletsh (Zee-Hot-Far-Floch-Tin-Ah-Koy-Letch) excl. - Describing someone who is mired in a kind of slump. The kind of slump where they are not getting any *action*, if you know what I mean...

Zudnik (Zood-Nik) n. - The buttocks (of the **tuchas**).

Chapter Twelve

WISE YIDDISH PROVERBS

"Give a man a fish and feed him for a day. Don't teach a man to fish and feed yourself. He's a grown man and fishing's not that hard.

*Nick Offerman as Ron Swanson, **Parks and Recreation***

The Yiddish language comes with its fair share of wisdom. Some of the greatest minds have spoken Yiddish: Mordecai Goldstein, Shmuel Klein, Ester Goldenberg, Miriam Abramovitz. These are just a few of the names of the great minds in my weekly Torah study.

A nar iz zayn eygener moser - A fool is his own informer.

A halber emes iz a gantser lign - A half truth is a whole lie. This is a good one to tell your kids when you want to give them an example of something that doesn't apply to every situation. Your sister's makeup looks terrible on her prom day? Then the half truth becomes the whole truth!

Oyb got volt gelebt af der erd voltn mentshn tsebrokhn zayne fentster - If God lives on earth, people would break down His windows. Our wise Jewish ancestors wanted us to remember that even if you believe in our monistic creator, you hopefully realize that not every prayer will be answered.

Oyb mazl ruft, shlogt zey for avekzetsn - If fortune calls, offer them a seat. Don't miss out on opportunities in life when you are faced with them. I sometimes lie awake at night thinking about how Rebecca, the hottest girl in our middle school, turned out to have a crush on me and I never did anything about it. I should've offered her a seat.

Di meydl vos ken nisht tantsn zogt az di kapelye ken nisht shpiln - The girl who can't dance says the band can't play. In Jewish culture, it is important to remind yourself that you have to take responsibility for your actions instead of passing blame. Like that time at summer camp, I threw sand at a kid's face and blamed it on the wind. But I got away with it, so what does that say for this proverb?

Fun glik tsu umglik iz nor a shrift; fun umglik tsu mazl iz a langer veg - From fortune to misfortune is but a step; from misfortune to fortune is a long way. Basically, it's easy to lose everything but hard to get everything. Reminds me of when I worked all summer to save up for *Lightning McQueen* light-up crocs, just for them to stop working after a few months. Sometimes life isn't fair.

Mit gelt in keshene bistu klug un bist sheyn un du zingst oykh gut - With money in your pocket, you are wise and you are handsome and you sing well too. I guess rich people get way more praise and are looked on more favorably. Think Jeff Bezos, Elon Musk, Donald Trump...well, perhaps the narrative has shifted since this proverb first came out.

Shikn a nar tsu farmakhn di lodn un er vet zey farmakhn zey iber der shtot - Send a fool to close the shutters and he'll close them all over town. I think this one is saying that people who are dumb are REALLY dumb. Maybe you could clarify to the fool to only close your shutters so we could avoid this mess altogether.

Tsayt iz der bester dokter - Time is the best doctor. Yet I have never gotten over Rebecca.

Ven ir zogt a gutn morgn tsu dem rebbe, zogt gut morgn aoykh tsu dem rebbes froy - When you say good morning to the **rebbe**, say good morning also to the **rebbe**'s wife. Just a reminder to be kind to everyone, whether they are the leader of your congregation or not.

Chapter Thirteen

APHORISMS

"Our business is infested with idiots who try to impress by using pretentious jargon."

David Ogilvy

At this point in the book, you're probably wondering what the difference between a proverb and an aphorism is. Very valid question. While a proverb is a metaphorical saying that provides vague advice based on someone's experience, an aphorism is a direct and literal phrase that expresses someone's opinion. Hope that clears things up a bit. If not, too bad.

Az me ken nit vi me vil, muz men vein vi me ken - If you can't do what you like, you must like what you can do. Our ancestors knew that finding an enjoyable career path is tough. Except for them, they had to pretty much decide between being a money lender, **mohel**, or **rebbe**.

Di kats hot lib fish, nor zi vil di fis nit ayn-netsn - The cat loves fish, but doesn't want to get her feet wet. Sometimes you just have to wade in the water and put in the work to get what you want. But sometimes the cat is independently wealthy enough to hire a company that will retrieve the fish for them. It's not the point of the aphorism but it is something to think about.

Ehren is fil tei'erer far gelt - Honor is dearer than money. Tell that to Bernie Madoff.

Eren iz fil tairer far gelt, nor keyn seychel nit - Money buys everything except common sense. Think about all the dumb wealthy people out there. There's too many to list.

Kinder un gelt iz a shaine velt - Children and money make a nice world. Simple yet poignant.

Mit gelt ken men nit shtoltsiren, me ken es laycht farliren! - Don't be boastful about money, it's easily lost. It's just not a good look.

Zog nisht keyn mol az du geyst dem letstn veg - Don't ever say you're traveling your last road. That never say die attitude that helped the Red Sox comeback 3-0 against the Yankees in 2004.

Chapter Fourteen

PLACING A CURSE ON YOUR WORST ENEMY

"Call it a curse, or just call me blessed. If you can't handle my worst, you ain't getting my best."

Nicki Minaj on "Marilyn Monroe"

Nothing says true hatred like putting a curse on your sworn enemy. For me, that person is the aforementioned Shlomi. I think I tried every curse in this chapter and then tried a few in some other languages. It worked in the end! He got broken up with one week before prom. You gotta feel a bit bad for the guy but at the same time, I felt like he might've had it coming.

A choleryeh af dir - I wish a plague on you.

A kleyn kind zol nokh im heysn - May a child be named after you soon. In Judaism, you cannot name a child after someone who is alive. See what they're getting at?

Lign in drerd un bakn beygl! - May you lie in the ground and bake bagels. It's a curse on your enemy to die and be cooked by the heat of hell, beside tasty-ass bagels they will never be able to eat.

Ale tseyn zoln bay im aroysfaln, nor eyner zol im blaybn oyf tsonveytik - May all your teeth fall out but one, so that you may still get a toothache. I have several dentist uncles if you need help with that.

Es zol dir dunern in boykh, vestu meyen az s'iz a homon klaper - Your stomach will rumble so badly, you'll think it was a *Purim* noisemaker. The noisemaker they're referring to is called a "gregger" and it is used when reading the story of *Purim*. Every time the villain's name, *Haman*, comes up in the story, everyone listening is supposed to shake the device as loud as they can.

Hindert hayzer zol er hobn, in yeder hoyz a hindert tsimern, in yeder tsimer tsvonsik betn un kadukhes zol im varfn fin eyn bet in der tsveyter - May you have a hundred houses, a hundred rooms in each house, 20 beds in each room, and may fever and chills toss you from one bed to the next. Oof.

Oyf doktoyrim zol er dos avekgebn - He should give his fortune away to all the doctors. Your biggest hater wants you in and out of the hospital until you run out of money. If only there was free healthcare.

Oyskrenkn zol er dus mames milakh - May he get so sick that he coughs up his own mother's milk.

Vi tsu derleb ikh im shoyn tsu bagrobn - I should outlive him long enough to see him buried. This one isn't even creative.

Zolst zayn azoy raykh, az dayn almone's man darf keynmol nisht arbetn a tog - May you be so rich your widow's husband has to never work a day. This one's a bit of a thinker. It says that I hope you die and your widow and their new partner enjoy your hard-earned cash.

Chapter Fifteen

JEWISH JOKES

"Clothes make the man. Naked people have little or no influence on society."

Mark Twain

The Jewish people have a storied history of legendary comedians. Groucho Marx, Lenny Bruce, Gilda Radner, George Burns, Jackie Mason, Mel Brooks, Sarah Silverman, Jerry Seinfeld, and Larry David to name a few. We even have *Borat* himself, Sasha Baron Cohen. Many believe Jewish people have gone into comedy as a way of coping with generations of persecution. I think it gives us an outlet to **kvetch** without being called a **yenta**.

The Beach Joke

A Jewish grandfather takes his grandchildren to the beach. The kids are playing in the sand when suddenly, a wave comes and pulls the smallest granddaughter into the water. Panicked, the grandfather prays to God. "Oh God, please bring her back and let her live!". Suddenly, an even bigger wave bursts out of the ocean, setting the little girl down right at his grandfather's feet. He scoops her up into a hug. Then he stares up at the sky and says, "She also had a hat."

Loving Mothers Joke

Three Jewish mothers are sitting on a bench, arguing over which of their sons loves them the most. The first one says, "You know, my son sends me flowers every Shabbos."
"You call that love?," says the second mother. "My son calls me every day!"
"That's nothing," says the third woman. "My son is in therapy five days a week. And the whole time, he talks about me!"

Israeli Joke

A group of people are standing on a subway platform — an American, a Russian, and an Israeli. A reporter approaches and says, "Excuse me, can I get your opinion about the meat shortage?"
"What's a shortage?" says the American.
"What's meat?" says the Russian.
"What's excuse me?" says the Israeli.

The Not-So-Kosher Joke

A **rebbe** is keeping a secret: she always wanted to try pork. One night, she drives through town to the furthest restaurant from her synagogue, ordering an entire suckling pig. As the waiter sets down the full roast pig, with an apple in its mouth, she sees a group of her congregants have walked in and are watching her. The **rebbe** widens her eyes, "What kind of place is this?!" she says. "You order an apple and look how it's served!"

Rat-Mitzvah joke

A synagogue has a mice problem. The janitor tries traps, bait, and everything in between but nothing works. Finally, he goes to the **rebbe** and explains the problem. "I have the solution," the **rebbe** says. "Well, what is it?" says the custodian. "It's a foolproof plan," the **rebbe** says, smiling. "I'll give them all bar and bat mitzvahs and we'll never see them again!"

Rowing Joke

A yeshiva decides to start a rowing team. But no matter how much they practice, they lose every single race. Eventually they decide to send one boy down to the nearby prep school as a spy, to watch their winning crew team and find out what their secret is. After a day of reconnaissance, the boy comes back. "Listen!" he tells his teammates. "I learned how they do it — they have eight guys rowing, and only <u>one</u> guy screaming!"

Chapter Sixteen

YIDDISH CULTURE FROM THE SILVER SCREEN

"Looks like I picked the wrong week to quit sniffing glue."

Lloyd Bridges as Steven McCroskey, **Airplane**

As the stars of stage and screen, Jewish people seem to own Hollywood!...I mean that in the figurative sense. Please don't use this to form a misguided perception of the Jews' role in the media. We do not control the media or Hollywood. If we did, you'd see more than six movies on this list.

We certainly have made a few films about life as a Jewish person. Many of these films even use slang from the Yiddish language! I encourage you to go check these out after finishing this chapter...or at least the good ones.

1) **An American Pickle (2020) -** Ah yes. The classic story of a man who falls into a vat of pickles and wakes up in the future (unfortunately not with super powers). And it's a Seth Rogen film!

New Slang
HaShem (Ha-Shem) n. - Not exactly slang but it is the way to say the name of the Lord outside of prayers.

My rating: 6/10
Two Seth Rogens was a few too many Seth Rogens for me. Definitely not his best work but still some funny moments and interesting points about differences in Jewish culture across generations.

2) **A Serious Man (2009)** - Experience the modern Jewish life with the Gopnik family. Spoiler alert: it's a bit miserable. Several scenes of Danny Gopnik, the main character's son, take me back to the good ol' days at my Jewish middle school.

New Slang
Dybbuk (Dee-Book) n. - This is an evil spirit from Jewish mythology. It is believed to possess and control the body of a deceased person.

Goy (Goy) n. - A word used to describe any person who is not Jewish.

Olam Ha-bah (Oh-Lahm-Ha-Bah) n. - Literally meaning the world to come. This refers to the Jewish afterlife.

My rating: 7.5
By far the best made movie on this list. Some incredible names in this movie too. Solomon Schultz, Dick Dutton, Larry Gopnik, etc. Altogether, an interesting Coen brothers film with a bit of a convoluted message.

3) **Fiddler on the Roof (1971) -** Traditionnnnn! Awesome movie musical. So what if it has a three hour run time! Maybe you should save it to watch while fasting on *Yom Kippur*.

New Slang
Shtetl (Shteh-Tull) n. - These were small Jewish market villages where my ancestors lived back in Eastern Europe.
Fun dayn moyl in Gott's oyern - From your mouth to God's ears. A classic expression that symbolizes hope and longing, such that your prayers will be heard by God. People are always questioning God's existence but I wonder what evidence we have to suggest he has ears.

Vaksn zolstu vi a tsibele mitn kop in dr'erd! - May you grow like an onion with its head in the ground. A famous Yiddish curse. If you want to be a little meaner you can add, "...with your feet in the hospital."

My rating: 7/10
Another interesting look into life in the **shtetl**, some older Jewish traditions, and the way cultural assimilation shaped their lives. Honestly, this movie did not need to be three hours but still a great film with tons of fun songs.

4) **The Producers (1967) -** Written and directed by legendary Jewish filmmaker, Mel Brooks! This film depicts a flailing producer who teams up with his accountant to make a broadway production that is a flop. This would allow them to keep the money for themselves and away from the investors. So these two Jews set out to make a musical about Hitler.

New Slang
Bialy (Bee-Ah-Lee) n. - Part of a character's last name, this is a type of Polish bread roll, sometimes compared to a bagel.

Bris (Briss) n. - Also the last name of a character, referring to the aforementioned ceremony conducted by the **mohel**, where the foreskin is *snip snipped*.

My rating: 6.5/10
Certainly not the best musical film on this list. While all the songs are still incredible, some of the bits just didn't age that well.

5) **Shiva Baby (2020) -** While at a **Shiva**, Danielle interacts with a variety of neurotic, narcissistic, and all-around strange individuals. This is pretty much what large Jewish functions feel like, with **yenta** relatives, friends, or exes prying into your life.

   New Slang
   Shiva (Shih-Vah) n. - The Jewish mourning reception that typically takes place at the family of the deceased's house.

   Kaput (Kah-Put) adj. - Something that is broken, done-for, or completely useless.

   My rating: 7/10
   70 mins of high stress and anxiety jam-packed into this little film. But a very funny insight into how our culture can be toxic.

6) **The Frisco Kid (1979) -** A silly, fun, and interesting representation of orthodox Jewish culture. Lots of Yiddish spoken in it, including the first lines of the film.

   New Slang
   Oy vey is mir (Oy-Vay-Iss-Meer) excl. - An overly dramatic phrase that translates to, "I am pain itself".

   My rating: 8.5/10
   What a journey between a Rabbi and a bank robber. Ultimately, I loved it. So charming, wholesome, with a tremendous amount of Yiddish slang.

Chapter Seventeen

YIDDISH EXPRESSIONS TO LIVE BY

"Well, I don't know how many years on this Earth I got left. I'm gonna get real weird with it."

Danny Devito as Frank Reynolds, **It's Always Sunny in Philadelphia**

As we move to the end of the book, what more fitting of a chapter then Yiddish expressions to live by. These expressions can help guide you down the path to success and happiness. And before you say it, expressions, aphorism, and proverbs are all very different things. Don't make me explain it again. It will make me upset and I've already had a very stressful day.

Abi gezunt - Meaning "As long as you have your health". Don't worry too much about what you can't control, at least you're still healthy. Easier said than done when every Jewish person I know has anxiety, including myself.

A brokh! - What you yell when there is a disaster: "Oh damn!".

A chazzer bleibt a chazzer - A pig will always remain a pig. To say that someone who is greedy will always continue to be greedy. I once had a real **chazzer** of a boss who wouldn't let us do casual Fridays. One day I said screw it and showed up to work in my pajamas, slippers, and sleepy-time nightcap...and I got fired. Turns out you have to wear a vest, helmet, and steel-toe boots if you're gonna work on a construction site.

A gezunt dir in pupik - Good health to your belly button. It is a sarcastic remark to say "thanks for absolutely nothing". Say it to your friend who bought hotdog buns for the barbecue when you're making hamburgers. Guess you're gonna have to get creative.

A gezunt oyf dein kop! - Good health on your head! The Yiddish language loves expressions that mention the **kop** (head).

Der mensch trakht un Gott lahkht - Man plans and God laughs. Things don't always go as planned in life. I never thought I'd be able to own property before my thirties! And I still don't!

Du zolst nicht visn fun tsores - You should never know from misery or trouble. It is an expression to say to someone to hope they never have to deal with anything bad or difficult in their lives. We all know this is unrealistic but it's a nice thought. You probably expected a joke or anecdote here but I just wanted to wish the best for all of you currently reading this chapter. It's a tough world out there!

Ess vet zich oys-hailen far der chasseneh - It will heal in time for the wedding. Similar to **Tseyt iz der bester dokter** (time is the best doctor), but a bit more specific. A wedding is one of the most joyous occasions in Judaism. Some of my favorite Jewish wedding traditions include:

- The bride and groom smash a glass to symbolize the destruction of the Temple in 70 CE.
- All the guests yell, "**Mazel Tov!**" in unison.
- After the ceremony, there is a celebratory dance called **The Hora**, which involves dancing in a circle. The bride, groom, and family members are lifted on chairs in the middle. It can get a bit violent.

Gay kocken offen yom - Go sh*t in the ocean. Like telling someone to go take a hike but with an added flavor.

Kein ayina hora - Literally meaning "No Evil Eye". It is a blessing to put at the end of a sentence of wishing someone well. You can even use it to bless things that will never happen. "May your $100 Super Bowl bet on the Dallas Cowboys come true, **kein ayina hora.**"

Nisht duggehdakht - May it never happen here. This is said in response to misery. "Did you hear they drink milk from bags in Canada? **Nisht duggehdakht.**"

Nisht gefehrlach - I've seen worse, this is not so terrible. This is the exact thing I said when I found out that Shlomi started dating my crush. I was devastated but it wasn't the first or worst he'd ever backstabbed me.

Nit azoy ai-ai-ai - That's not so good. Said about something that is underwhelming. According to my dad, this is the exact expression my Zaidy said to him when he watched the *Seinfeld* finale. Till today, I've watched every single episode except that last one.

Ongeshtopt mit gelt - One who is stuffed to the brim with money. Like the creator of the *Snuggie*™, Scott Boilen, who is now worth over $200 million. All that for a blanket that you can wear.

Chapter Eighteen

YIDDISH BITS THAT DIDN'T SEEM TO FIT ANYWHERE ELSE

"Random!"

*Tim Robinson as Hot Dog Guy, **I Think You Should Leave***

There's so many great Yiddish slang words out there that I just had to make sure I got them all. But don't get it twisted. This chapter isn't an island of misfit toys, it's the Yiddish Miscellaneous Hall of Fame.

Alrightnik (All-Rite-Nick) n. - A person who has successfully gone from low status and poor to high status and wealthy. The old rags to riches story is crucial in Jewish culture. Having so many relatives who started in the **shtetl**, it's important to recognize the come-up.

Big macher (Big-Mah-Cher) n. - A big shot. Someone who is making money-moves. This is the type of term you could use to make fun of a finance bro. "Oh look at the **big macher** over there. I can't believe he's networking at Great Uncle Terry's **shiva**."

Bist meshugeh? (Beest-Meh-Shoo-Geh) excl. - To ask someone, "are you crazy?". I remember when *I* lost my mind. There was something so pleasant about that place.

Did you think I was talking about myself? Sorry if it wasn't clear, those are actually lyrics from the 2006 hit *Crazy* by Gnarls Barkley. I don't know what Gnarls is talking about but I recommend checking the song out if you like mid 2000s alternative R&B.

Chai kock on a stick (Chai-Kock-On-Ah-Stik) expr. - Literally meaning eighteen (chai) pieces of cuck (poop) on a stick. So it's absolute crap that cannot be disguised as anything else. A liberal arts degree, for example.

Chas v'sholem! (Chas-Ve-Shah-Lem) excl. - To yell, "Heaven forbid it!". Here's some examples of things I'd want Heaven to forbid:
- Getting a cold when you're going to a wedding the next day
- Godzilla attacks when you're on your way to a wedding
- Fruit salad where the cantaloupe gets its flavor all over the other fruits (at a wedding)

Gevaldikeh zakh! (Geh-Val-Deh-Keh-Zakh) expr. - To sarcastically say a terrible thing has just happened. Use this when your sister is complaining about her cheeseburger coming with pickles, despite her asking for no pickles. Jess, you can just pick off the pickles. There's a bit of pickle residue but you'll survive.

Halevai! (Hah-Leh-Vai) excl. - If only! An exclamation that hopes something so desperately. To see someone using the slang from this book, **Halevai!**

Kholileh (Cho-Lee-Leh) excl. - Don't even think about it happening! Something that superstitious Jews would say, which is basically all of us.

Lebedickeh mensch (Leh-Beh-Dik-Eh-Mensh) n. - A lively and high spirited person. Someone who might make a great addition to a party. Larry David would say that they would make a great "middle".

Loch in kop (Loch-Een-Kop) n. - [I need this like] a hole in the head. Tax season coming up? Got a cold? Get concussed from an unfortunate trampoline accident? These are the kind of things that you certainly don't want, let alone need.

Oy gevalt! (Oy-Geh-Valt) excl. - Oh my God! A variation of **Oy-Vey** or **Oy-yoy-yoy**.

Plotz (Plotz) v. - To explode with emotion. Typically from anger or joy.

Shlep (Shlep) v. - This term means to drag or carry around. It is one of those terms that are very versatile. You can say, "In the 4th quarter, NBA star Joel Embiid could barely **shlep** his **tuchas** up and down the court because he was so tired." Or if you're not into sports it could be as simple as, "I **shlepped** the groceries all the way from the store and then remembered I forgot the eggs."

Oh my god –
is that Coconut?
I'm allergic to coconut.

MARRY ME?

YIDDISH BITS THAT DIDN'T SEEM TO FIT ANYWHERE ELSE

Shluf (Shloof) n. - To go to bed. To get a good night's rest. A perfect Yiddish word.

Shmatte (Shmah-Teh) n. - An old tattered rag. While this might seem like it has minimal usage, it is actually one of the most commonly used Yiddish words. It can refer to any piece of fabric or clothing that is ugly and ratty. It gets the point across pretty quick.

Shnoz (She-Nahz) n. - The **shnoz** is none other than the nose. Sometimes it's used to describe a huge, ugly one. But I say not anymore! It's time to reclaim the big nose. Imagine this: a world where people are getting plastic surgery to make their noses look bigger, and more stereotypically Jewish. Utopia.

Shtik (Shtik) n. - This goofy sounding word refers to someone's gimmick, performance, or routine. A **shtick** is often repetitive and it causes people to roll their eyes. "Oh there's Moishe, and he has the same old shtick about spraining his pinky". A **shtick** can also be a performer's act. Jerry Seinfeld's **shtick** would typically start with, "What's the deal with...?" and end with him lamenting about airline food, relationships, or whatever is bothering him today.

Shvitz (Sheh-Vitz) v. - Quite simply, it means sweating. Such a key part of Yiddish and Jewish culture, and a great final term for this book. Jews are notoriously strong sweaters. It doesn't even have to be related to exerting energy or being stressed. Alternatively, a **shvitz** can refer to a sauna filled with old, naked men.

Memories from Jewish Day School

Since we're here in the random section, I figured I could write about pretty much anything. I wanted to tell you about some of the best, funniest, worst, and weirdest memories I can recall from my time at Jewish day school.

- *1st Grade:* My friend Ben, unprovoked, took out a pair of scissors and cut a hole in his shirt. Ripped shirts weren't in style back then so it was weird.
- *2nd Grade:* Towards the end of the day, the girl beside me mentioned she wasn't feeling so good. She proceeded to throw up all over my arm.
- *3rd Grade:* A teacher threw a chair at one of my classmates. Luckily she didn't have great aim.
- *4th Grade:* Made a model of the city of Jerusalem using clay. We were then supposed to use podge to seal it but mistakenly used white glue. We called it "Jerusalem in the winter".
- *5th Grade:* We had a teacher who hated when we got up from our desk to throw out garbage during class time. We designated a time for everyone in the class to get up and throw out our trash at the same time as an act of rebellion. He was pissed.
- *6-8th Grade:* We got four Hebrew teachers to quit, move schools, or take a "forced sabbatical".

CONCLUSION

"I've got to get out of here. This is all wrong!"

Larry David

Well we did it! What a journey this was for both of us. You learned so many Yiddish phrases and I learned so much about myself. I think writing this book has been more valuable than therapy.

Thank you for reading! I encourage you to take what you've learned, and give your Zaidy and Bubbie a call, trying to finagle in as many new terms as you can into the conversation. Plus, I know they'd love to hear from you!

Finally, your feedback is invaluable to us! If you're enjoying "Yiddish Slang 101," please take a moment to leave a review. Share your thoughts, and consider adding a photo or video to enhance your review.

Your input helps others discover the beauty of Yiddish. Follow this link to leave your review (or scan the QR code):

Amazon.com/review/create-review?&asin=1915836964

Thank you for being a part of our Yiddish journey.

Warm regards,

Matthew
Author, "Oy Vey! Yiddish Slang 101"

THE BIG OL' YIDDISH GLOSSARY

A brokh!, page 84

A chazzer bleibt a chazzer , page 85

A choleryeh af dir, page 74

A gezunt dir in pupik, page 85

A gezunt oyf dein kop!, page 85

A halber emes iz a gantser lign, page 69

A kleyn kind zol nokh im heysn, page 74

A nar iz zayn eygener moser, page 69

Abi gezunt, page 84

Achalti otah, page 51

Achi, page 51

Ale tseyn zoln bay im aroysfaln, nor eyner zol im blaybn oyf tsonveytik, page 75

Alrightnik, page 87

Alter kocher, page 15

Arse, page 51

Az me ken nit vi me vil, muz men vein vi me ken, page 72

Balagan, page 52

Baleboste, page 35

Bashert, page 35

Beimaschah, page 52

Benzonah, page 52

Bialy, page 82

Big macher, page 88
Bissel, page 41
Bist meshugeh?, page 88
Bris, page 82
Bubaleh, page 41
Bubbie, page 36
Bupkis, page 8
Chachlah, page 52
Chag sameach, page 55
Chas v'sholem!, page 89
Chazzer, page 16
Chevrusa, page 28
Cholent, page 41
Chuch/Chuchie, page 37
Chutzpah, page 28
Der Mensch trakht un Gott lahkht, page 85
Di kats hot lib fish, nor zi vil di fis nit ayn-netsn, page 72
Di meydl vos ken nisht tantsn zogt az di kapelye ken nisht shpiln, page 70
Doogri, page 52
Du zolst nicht visn fun tsores, page 85
Dummkopf, page 25
Dybbuk, page 81
Ehren is fil tei'erer far gelt!, page 73
Eppes a nudnik, page 10
Eren iz fil tairer far gelt, nor keyn seychel nit, page 73
Erotoman, page 60
Es zol dir dunern in boykh, vestu meyen az s'iz a homon klaper, page 75
Ess vet zich oys-hailen far der chasseneh, page 85
Eynnakhtl, page 60
Farbisseneh punim, page 16
Farchtunken, page 17
Farputst, page 29
Farshlepteh krenk, page 10
Farshtinkener, page 17
Feh!, page 10
Ferklempt, page 46
Fershimmeled, page 17

Fershtickt, page 10
Fonferer, page 25
Fun dayn moyl in Gott's oyern, page 82
Fun glik tsu umglik iz nor a shrift; fun umglik tsu mazl iz a langer veg, page 70
Furshlugginer, page 11
Gantzeh mispocha, page 37
Gay kocken offen yom, page 86
Geshmak, page 30
Gevaldikeh zakh, page 89
Gikhele, page 61
Gmar chatima toyva, page 55
Goy, page 81
Gut yontif, page 55
Halevai!, page 89
Hamantaschen, page 42
HaShem, page 81
Hindert hayzer zol er hobn, in yeder hoyz a hindert tsimern, in yeder tsimer tsvonsik betn un kadukhes zol im varfn fin eyn bet in der tsveyter, page 75
Hitsiger, page 26
Ibbegeblibenis, page 42
Kaliber, page 52
Kaput, page 83
Karger, page 26
Kashe-bulbe, page 42
Kein ayina hora, page 86
Kholileh, page 89
Kibbitz, page 47
Kinder un gelt is a shaine velt, page 73
Kish mir in tuchas, page 62
Kishkas, page 42
Klutz, page 18
Kugel, page 42
Kvell, page 29
Kvetch, page 11
L'Chaim!, page 29
Lebedickeh mensch, page 89
Leeftafetz, page 52

Libe-feter, page 63
Lign in drerd un bakn beygl!, page 75
Loch in kop, page 89
Mah ani ez?!, page 52
Makhasheyfe, page 18
Mamaloshen, page 38
Mamzer, page 18
Matzo ball soup, page 42
Mazel tov!, page 49
Mensch, page 31
Meshugganeh, page 12
Mishegoss, page 12
Mit gelt in keshene bistu klug un bist sheyn un du zingst oykh gut, page 70
Mit gelt ken men nit shtoltsiren, me ken es laycht farliren!, page 73
Mohel, page 56
Naches, page 33
Nisht duggehdakht, page 86
Nisht gefehrlach, page 86
Nit azoy ai-ai-ai, page 86
Nochshlepper, page 18
Noder, page 53
Nogoodnik, page 19
Nosh, page 43
Nu?, page 49
Nudnik, page 18
Olam Ha-bah, page 81
Ongepotchket, page 13
Ongeshtopt mit gelt, page 86
Onknipverter, page 64
Oy gevalt!, page 90
Oy vey is mir, page 83
Oy vey!, page 13
Oy-yoy-yoy!, page 13
Oyb got volt gelebt af der erd voltn mentshn tsebrokhn zayne fentster, page 70
Oyb mazl ruft, shlogt zey for avekzetsn, page 70
Oyf doktoyrim zol er dos avekgebn, page 75

Oyskrenkn zol er dus mames milakh, page 75
Paskudnyak, page 19
Pisher, page 26
Pishkeh, page 33
Pisk, page 26
Plotz, page 90
Polutsye, page 65
Potch in tuchus, page 65
Putz, page 19
Rebbe, page 56
Rugelach, page 43
Sababa, page 53
Sachi, page 54
Schlemiel, page 23
Schlimazel, page 23
Schmaltz, page 44
Schmendrik, page 22
Schmooze, page 47
Schmuck, page 20
Schnorrer, page 26
Sh'koyech, page 57
Shana tova, page 56
Shande, page 20
Shayna punim, page 38
Shikn a nar tsu farmakhn di lodn un er vet zey farmakhn zey iber der shtot, page 70
Shiva, page 83
Shluf, page 92
Shlumperdik, page 21
Shmatte, page 92
Shmoe, page 22
Shofar, page 57
Shtetl, page 82
Shtik, page 92
Shtup, page 65
Shvitz, page 93
Simchah, page 57
Sufganiyot, page 44
Tachlis, page 49

Tatelah, page 38
Tizku leshanim rabot, page 57
Tseyt iz der bester dokter, page 70
Tsuris, page 13
Tsutsiik, page 66
Tuchas leker, page 22
Tuchas, page 66
Umbashrien, page 14
Vaksn zolstu vi a tsibele mitn kop in dr'erd!, page 82
Ven ir zogt a gutn morgn tsu dem rebbe, zogt gut morgn aoy-
kh tsu dem rebbes froy, page 71
Vi tsu derleb ikh im shoyn tsu bagrobn, page 75
Ya wah adi, page 54
Yalla!, page 54
Yenta, page 49
Yiddishe kop, page 34
Yutz/Yutzi, page 50
Zaidy, page 39
Zeyer sheyn gezogt, page 34
Zhlub, page 22
Zi hot farflokhtn a koyletsh, page 68
Zog nisht keyn mol az du geyst dem letstn veg, page 73
Zolst zayn azoy raykh, az dayn almone's man darf keynmol
nisht arbetn a tog, page 75
Zudnik, page 68

References

Goldman, E. A. (2021, March 8). *The 10 essential films of the Yiddish renaissance*. The Forward.

Kunza, J. (2022, February 11). *Our favorite over the top Yiddish curses*. Unpacked.

Kutzik, J. (2014, June 11). *How do you talk dirty in Yiddish?*. The Forward.

Magdalena, P. S. (2022). *Yiddish language and culture and its post-Holocaust fate in Europe*.

Miller, Y. A. (2023, May 2). *Great yiddish words, expressions, phrases & sayings*. Aish.com.

Singer, J. A. (2019, April 4). *The 10 Best, Most Classic Jewish Jokes*. The Forward.

University of Illinois Staff. (n.d.). *Why study yiddish?*. Germanic Languages and Literatures at Illinois.

Winston-Macauley, M. (2021, December 19). *The Yiddish curse*. Aish.com